Daniel and Max Play Together

Adapted by Amy Rosenfeld-Kass

Based on the screenplay written by Becky Friedman

Poses and layouts by Jason Fruchter

Simon Spotlight

New York   London   Toronto   Sydney   New Delhi

SIMON SPOTLIGHT
An imprint of Simon & Schuster Children's Publishing Division
1230 Avenue of the Americas, New York, New York 10020
This Simon Spotlight edition December 2021
© 2021 The Fred Rogers Company.
All rights reserved, including the right of reproduction in whole or in part in any form.
SIMON SPOTLIGHT and colophon are registered trademarks of Simon & Schuster, Inc.
For information about special discounts for bulk purchases, please contact Simon &
Schuster Special Sales at 1-866-506-1949 or business@simonandschuster.com.
Manufactured in the United States of America 1121 LAK
10 9 8 7 6 5 4 3 2 1
ISBN 978-1-5344-9700-9
ISBN 978-1-5344-9701-6 (ebook)

"Hi, neighbor! I just got to school," says Daniel Tiger.
He puts his backpack and lunch box into his cubby.
"Come on over for Circle Time," Teacher Harriet calls.

Next to Teacher Harriet is someone new. His name is Max. He wiggles, fidgets with his watch, and looks down at the floor.

"Max is my nephew, and I am his aunt," Teacher Harriet says.

"You're an aunt?" Prince Wednesday asks.

"I'm an aunt and a teacher," she says. "Max is visiting me, so I wanted him to meet all of you."

The children are excited to meet Max! They all want to say hello at the same time.

Max covers his ears, rocking back and forth. "That's too loud for Max," Teacher Harriet says. She puts a heavy blanket around Max's shoulders. It makes him feel like he's getting a nice, cozy hug.

"But why does Max need a blanket? Is he cold?" Daniel asks.

"Max is not cold," Teacher Harriet says. "Max is autistic. Some things about him are different, like the way he calms down."

Then she pulls out a book. "Max, now that you are feeling calmer, are you ready to show them the book we made together?"

"That's my book," Max says, pointing.

Teacher Harriet opens the book and reads, "'Max is visiting school and meeting new friends.'"

Max points to the pictures of Daniel and his classmates on the page. One by one, he says their names out loud.

"Hey, that's me!" Daniel exclaims.

"He knows our names, hoo hoo!" O the Owl cheers.

O the Owl

Prince Wednesday

Miss Elaina

Daniel Tiger

Katerina Kittycat

Jodi Platypus

Max covers his ears again when he hears the loud voices. "If Max covers his ears, it is too loud for him," Teacher Harriet explains. "You can move back to give him more space and talk in a soft voice. Right, Max?"

Max nods, taking his hands off his ears.

"Something that might sound okay to you might be too loud for Max," Teacher Harriet says. She sings,

"When a friend needs different things than you, there are some things you can do."

Teacher Harriet continues to read the book. "'Max needs time before he is ready to play with new friends. He likes to share the things he is interested in, like bugs and buses.'"

Max looks closely at the book to see the pictures. "That's a roly-poly bug! Roly-poly bugs curl up into a ball when they feel scared," he says.

Max suddenly leaves Circle Time and walks over to the window.

"Can Max come back?" Miss Elaina asks. "I want him to tell us more about bugs!"

"Max needs time to get comfortable in the classroom," Teacher Harriet says. "I'm going to let him look out the window while we finish Circle Time."

"'Max and his new friends have a great day at school. The End,'" Teacher Harriet reads. Then she puts the book down and says, "Now it's Choice Time."

Max goes to the block corner for Choice Time. "Can I play with you?" Daniel asks. But Max doesn't look up.

Daniel pulls out some blocks. Then he gets closer to Max and asks again, "Do you want to build a castle with me?" Max doesn't answer.

"I like playing buses, city buses, school buses, and double-decker buses," Max says.

"I like playing buses too, but right now I'm building a castle," Daniel replies. "See?"

"If I went on a double-decker bus, I would sit on top," Max says without looking up.

"Why does Max keep talking about buses?" Daniel asks. "Sometimes, when Max is really excited about something, he only wants to talk about that one thing," Teacher Harriet says. "If Max wants to talk about buses, does it mean he can't play with me?" Daniel asks. "I really want to play with him!"

"Maybe you can play something you both like," Teacher Harriet says.

 "When a friend needs different things than you, there are some things you can do."

Then Daniel has an idea. "I like building, and Max likes buses. So I can build a bus station!"

Max looks at Daniel's bus station and drives his bus closer.

"Max *does* want to play with me!" Daniel says. He opens the gate of the bus station and shouts, "Right on schedule! *Clang, clang, clang!*"

Max covers his ears, and Daniel remembers that some things are too loud for Max, even if it sounds okay to him. Daniel whispers in a softer voice, *"Clang, clang, clang!"*

After a while, Katerina Kittycat and O the Owl walk by. "Would you like to come to our tea party?" they ask, handing Daniel an invitation.

"I'll come," Daniel replies. When they begin to walk away, he calls out, "Wait! You forgot to invite Max."

"I thought Max only wanted to play with buses," says Katerina. "But maybe . . . he wants to play tea party too!" She gives him an invitation.

After a while, Max drives his bus out of the block area and toward Katerina and O. He wants to play tea party too . . . just in his own way!

"Welcome to the tea party!" Katerina says.

"Right on schedule!" Daniel says.

"Right on schedule," Max echoes.

"When a friend needs different things than you, there are some things you can do,"

Daniel sings. "I like my new friend, Max. I'm glad I did some different things so we could play together. Ugga Mugga!"

Dear reader,

When I was a child, I had a learning disability. I played with the friends who accepted me for who I was and also wanted to play with me.

It took me a while to warm up to new friends. I also liked playing with one or two friends instead of in a big group.

Once I felt comfortable around them, though, we had a lot of fun! Sometimes we got dressed up like adults and pretended to have tea parties like our parents. Other times we played "house." I wore my mom's shoes and sat on the couch with tea, just like she did! We also did arts and crafts together: drawing, painting, and collage.

I also liked playing that I was a teacher. Michael, my brother and friend, and Shari, my best friend, were students.

Now that I am grown up, I am a professional teacher and educator! In my career, I have worked with children in Early Intervention programs. I have also traveled to different schools as a Special Education teacher. I have learned that all children are different and learn in their own special ways.

After work, I like to do so many different activities with my friends, like going to museums, theaters, restaurants, and movies.

Your family can be your friends too. My husband, Gary, is one of my best friends. We like to travel together. My dad, stepmom, and brother-in-law are all my friends too!

What do you like to do with your friends? Remember, it is okay to be different. You can play and learn in your own special way!

—Amy Rosenfeld-Kass